# BATWHEELS
**DC**™

# HERE COMES REDBIRD!

by Billy Wrecks

Batman created by Bob Kane with Bill Finger

Random House 🏠 New York

Bam and Redbird are
practicing their moves
in the Batcave.
Redbird flips over Bam!
"Great work!" says Bam.

The team cheers!
Bam and Redbird
bump tires and say,
"Our wheels are turning,
and our rubber
is burning!"

Suddenly, they hear
an alarm.
The Joker is robbing
a bank in Gotham City!

The heroes Batman
and Robin buckle up.
Redbird is too young.
He is left behind.

Bam and the heroes
get going!
They must stop
The Joker.

*VROOM!*

They chase The Joker. The Super-Villain sees them!

Redbird joins the chase,
even though he should
stay in the Batcave.

The Joker launches
Bursty Bombs at them
from Prank, his van.
It bounces off Redbird
and splatters Bam!

Bam crashes!
Batman and Robin
will continue on foot.

Redbird is sorry
he caused the crash.
Bam says they
have to stop Prank.

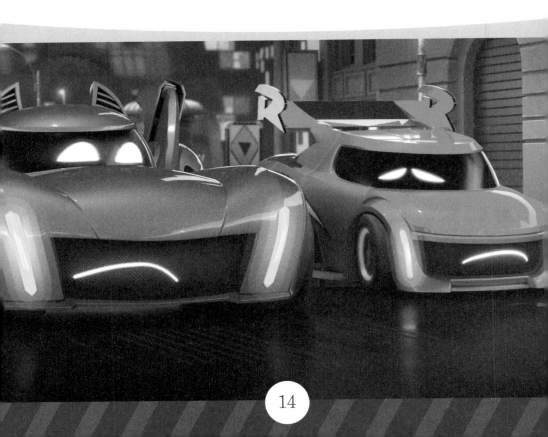

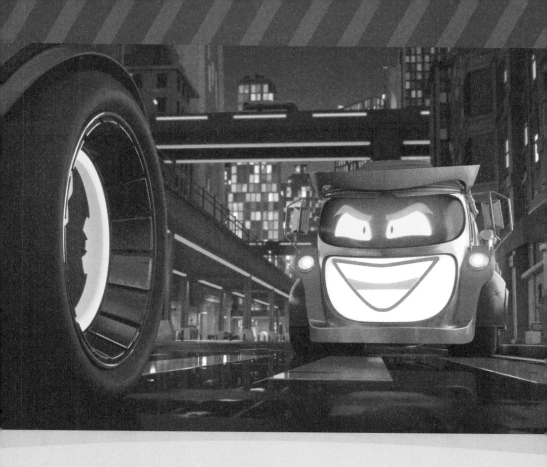

They try to sneak up
on Prank, but the van
hears Redbird.
Prank laughs.

Prank dodges
Bam's trap.
He races off.

But he will not get away!
Bam and Redbird
engage the Bat-link
to share power, and . . .

. . . *VROOM!*

They take off!

Redbird flips over Prank!
It is the same move
he used in the Batcave.

Prank is shocked—
when Redbird zaps
him with The Joker's
joy buzzer!

Prank is out
of commission.
The Joker does not
have a getaway
van now!

Batman easily
catches The Joker—
and has the last laugh.

"Our wheels are turning,
and our rubber
is burning!"
Bam and Redbird shout.
Redbird is now
a great sidekick!

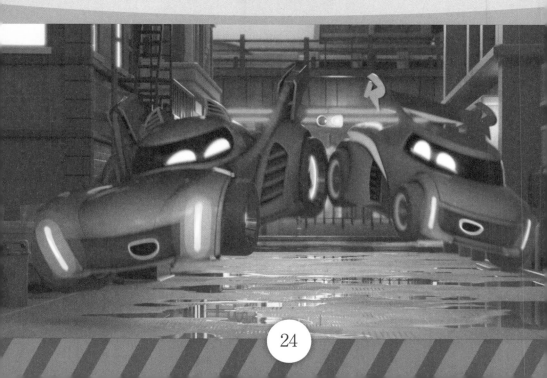